Downl Fever

Written by Jonny Zucker
Illustrated by Lee Wildish

Titles in Full Flight 4

Download Fever	Jonny Zucker
TV heat	Jonny Zucker
Mer-boy	Justine Smith
Rock Chick	Jillian Powell
Handbag Wars	Jillian Powell
Dark Star	Melanie Joyce
Kelly's Diary	Helen Orme
Striking Out	Jane West
Mystery in Mexico	Jane West
Snowboard Adventure	Alison Milford

Badger Publishing Limited
15 Wedgwood Gate, Pin Green Industrial Estate,
Stevenage, Hertfordshire SG1 4SU
Telephone: 01438 356907. Fax: 01438 747015
www.badger-publishing.co.uk
enquiries@badger-publishing.co.uk

Download Fever ISBN 1 84691 029 3
ISBN 978-1-84691-029-6

Series Editor: Jonny Zucker
Publisher: David Jamieson
Commissioning Editor: Carrie Lewis
Editor: Paul Martin
Design: Fiona Grant
Illustration: Lee Wildish

Download Fever

Contents

Brand New

Keisha had just got a ZZone mp3 player. The ZZone had just come out. It was sleek and blue. Keisha had saved up for months to buy it.

It sounded even better than it had in the shop.

Her best mate Shelly came over to check it out.

"That is *so* cool," grinned Shelly. "Give us a go."

They hung out for two hours, listening to music and talking about Keisha's new mp3 player.

That night Keisha slept with the ZZone on her bedside table.

She slept very deeply.

So she didn't see the weird flashing letters and numbers that appeared on its screen in the middle of the night.

Weird Message

On the bus to school the next morning, Keisha listened to music on her ZZone.

She showed it to all of her mates before school.

At lunch break, she was on her way to meet up with Shelly when she heard a tiny beeping sound coming from her ZZone.

She pulled it out of her pocket. On the screen was a line of letters and numbers:

Ldj6rey092wsoi55snxdio7dnfh63jdetwej9

"What's up?" called Shelly.

Keisha looked up.

Shelly was walking towards her.

Keisha checked the screen again.

“I just saw some funny letters and numbers on my ZZone,” Keisha said.

Shelly looked at the blank screen.

“They were only there for a few seconds,” Keisha said.

Shelly pulled a face. "It must be because it's new. Come on, let's go."

Keisha checked the screen again and then hurried after Shelly.

When Keisha got home after school, she looked in the booklet that had come with the ZZone.

There was nothing about rows of letters and numbers appearing.

Maybe Shelly was right. New machines often did weird things.

Later, when she was watching TV, her ZZone made the tiny beeping sound again.

Some words appeared on the screen:

Ready **Start** **Soon**

Keisha frowned. What did the words mean? *Ready* to *start* what *soon*?

Then the words vanished.

An hour later, Keisha was trying out a new red top in her bedroom. She was thinking *how good would it be not to go to school tomorrow?*

At that second she heard the ZZone beep. She ran over to her table and picked it up.

On the screen it said:
How good would it be not to go to school tomorrow?

Keisha stared at the screen in horror. She dropped the ZZone on the floor.

SALE

Fall Out

“Is this a wind up?” asked Shelly.

It was the next morning. The girls were sitting on a wall just outside school. It was ten minutes before the bell went.

“I swear,” replied Keisha. “I was thinking how good it would be to miss school today then, two seconds later, the screen said the same thing.”

"You're scaring me," said Shelly. “Maybe it was just a dream.”

“It wasn’t a dream,” said Keisha crossly.

“Well, is it in the memory? Can I see it?”

HIGH
SCHOOL

Keisha shook her head. “I can’t find it anywhere.”

“Maybe you’re just tired and you imagined it.”

“I didn’t imagine it!” Keisha snapped.

She jumped down off the wall and stormed off.

If Shelly didn’t believe her then what kind of friend was she?

It's For Real

After school Keisha went back to the shop where she'd bought the ZZone.

The man who sold it to her was there. She told him everything.

He looked as if he was going to laugh when she told him about her thoughts appearing on the screen.

He opened the player and looked inside. "It looks fine," he said. "There's nothing to worry about."

Keisha thought about phoning Shelly, but she was still angry with her.

The next day was Saturday. Keisha got up late and ate breakfast. She was just wishing she hadn't finished the cornflakes yesterday, when the ZZone beeped. She looked at the screen.

I wish I hadn't finished the cornflakes yesterday.

It was happening again!

At that second the doorbell went.

It was Shelly.

"Hey Keisha, I'm sorry."

Keisha stared at her mate. "It's okay," she said. "But it's all true."

"Can I have another look at the ZZone?" asked Shelly.

Keisha handed the ZZone over. Shelly stared at it.

At that moment some words appeared on the screen:

I want to believe Keisha but it does all sound too weird.

"Oh my god!" croaked Shelly.

The Lab

Keisha and Shelly hurried down the road.

Shelly had said they should go to the place where the ZZones were made.

A huge silver building loomed above them.

They pushed open the front door.

A guard was sitting behind a desk.

"We both need the loo," said Keisha. "And this is the only place that looked open."

The guard looked at them suspiciously.

"Okay," he said. "It's on the first floor. But be quick."

They got into the lift. On the wall was a sign listing all of the companies in the building.

Floor 7 said ZONE TECH.

Keisha pressed 7 and the lift moved up.

On Floor 7, a big sign read ZONE TECH.

The girls found themselves in a long white corridor.

At the end was a bright blue door.

They hurried down the corridor.

Keisha pushed the blue door open.

Inside was a huge lab. There were wires and machines everywhere.

A woman spun round in a chair.

"Keisha and Shelly," the woman said. "I've been expecting you."

The woman had short blond hair and cold, blue eyes. She wore a badge saying *Dr Grey*.

"How do you know our names?" asked Keisha.

"I know a lot more than your names," said Dr Grey.

"It's that mp3 player, isn't it?" asked Shelly.

Dr Grey nodded. "It just happened that Keisha was the person who bought the first, 'Special' ZZone," she said.

" 'Special', because it can read minds?" asked Keisha.

"Exactly," replied Dr Grey.

"*Why* do you want to read Keisha's mind?" asked Shelly.

Dr Grey laughed. "This isn't just about *Keisha.* Now I know the ZZone works, I'm going to flood the shops with them. And I'm going to make them much, much cheaper than all other mp3 players. Soon every teenager in the country will have one."

"Why?" asked Keisha.

"Can't you see?" sneered Dr Grey. "Soon I'll know what type of food, films, music and TV shows every teenager likes. Companies will pay me millions of pounds for that kind of information."

"That's really creepy," said Keisha.

PoP

"But that's not all," said Dr Grey. "It won't be long before I can do more than read your minds. Soon I'll be able to *put thoughts into your heads.*"

"What kind of thoughts?" asked Shelly with horror.

"Thoughts that *I* choose," replied Dr Grey. "It won't be long before I can control *all* of you."

"No way!" said Keisha.

"Yes way!" snapped Dr Grey. "You'll do what I tell you. If I want you to buy one type of chocolate bar, you'll buy it! If I want you to fight in a war, then you WILL fight in a war!"

"You're mad!" shouted Shelly.

"There's no way you can do it," said Keisha. "We're going to the police right now - they'll stop you."

"NO ONE WILL STOP ME!" shouted Dr Grey. "And you two won't be going anywhere!"

At that second, Keisha spotted a big red panel on the wall next to Dr Grey. It said SYSTEM SHUT DOWN.

Keisha pulled out her ZZone and threw it as hard as she could.

Dr Grey tried to catch it but missed. The ZZone smashed into the red panel.

"NO!" screamed Dr Grey. She ran over to a metallic desk and desperately started pushing rows of tiny black buttons. But she couldn't stop the explosion. Suddenly the lab was filled with smoke and a huge fireball appeared. The fire swallowed up Dr Grey.

But the fireball was heading for Keisha and Shelly.

“RUN!” screamed Keisha.

They ran towards the door. It was locked.

The fireball was getting nearer and nearer.

“HELP!” screamed Shelly.

At that second, Keisha saw some levers on the wall. She pulled them down one-by-one.

‘QUICK!’ yelled Shelly.

The fireball was nearly on them.

Keisha pulled down the last lever.

The door flew open. They sped out.

The girls ran down the stairs and out of the main door.

They kept running, until a giant explosion rocked the ground behind them.

They both dived onto the floor as the building was covered in flames and glass flew everywhere.

A Lucky Escape

"You were lucky," said the police woman.

Keisha and Shelly were in hospital with minor burns.

"You stopped Dr Grey's plan," said the police woman. "But if you ever sense danger in the future, please tell the police first, okay?"

Keisha and Shelly nodded.

Later that night, the girls were back at Keisha's house.

"Next time you buy an mp3 player," said Shelly, "take me with you."

"I knew you were going to say that," laughed Keisha. "I could read your mind!"

As Keisha and Shelly sat talking, a door at the back of the badly burned, silver building, was slowly pushed open.

A tall woman, with short blond hair and blue eyes, slipped outside. She was badly burnt but still alive. In her hand was a tiny microchip, marked *ZZone*.

She looked behind her and then disappeared into the night.